fools rush flynn

dog tags
book two

Kat Baxter

Fools Rush Flynn

Kat Baxter

Edited by: Emily Beierle-McKaskle

Copyeditor: BookReadingJenn

Book cover: Cormar Covers

Cover image: CJC Photography

Cover model: Dominic Calvani

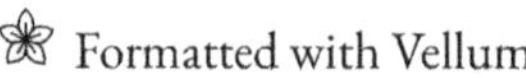
Formatted with Vellum

fools rush flynn

A FAKE MARRIAGE. Sizzling attraction. And only one bed.

Temple

Marrying my best friend's older brother was the perfect solution to my problem. Flynn was heading back overseas to serve in the military, and I got my inheritance. No complications. No messy emotions. Just signatures on paper and a gold band on my finger.

But when my cousin decides to contest my marriage, I know I need to find my "fake" husband and make our union look real.

. . .

Flynn

I did my duty—signed the papers, played the hero, and secured Temple's inheritance. It was easy to play the doting husband from across several oceans. But when I open my door to find my wife standing there, pink luggage in tow, I know my quiet life in Saddle Creek just got a whole lot louder.

Our marriage was only meant to be a means to an end. Now she's living in my one-bedroom cabin, testing every ounce of my self-control. I'm starting to think the biggest lie we ever told... was that this marriage wasn't real.

chapter **one**

TEMPLE

You know those kids... the ones that talk too much, laugh too loudly and need an extra amount of attention? Yeah, I'm one of those.

For as far back as I can remember, people—mostly family, but often teachers—have told me I need to take it down a notch. Or ten.

I'm sure there's some underlying reason that makes me take up more space than I should. Aside from the fact that as a plus sized woman I literally take up more physical space.

For a long time, I tried to conform to other people's expectations. Tried to be quieter, smaller, less colorful, and just less "too much".

But the truth is the more I try to suppress my natural instincts, the worse things get. So since I can't really change, I've learned to ration other people's exposure to me. Everyone likes me more in small doses.

Which means I know lots of people, and I have exactly one friend. A friend I haven't seen in ages because she's been doing a semester abroad which morphed into another semester and then another. I miss her dreadfully.

And then there's Flynn Harrington. My girlhood crush. My bestie's hot, older brother. And currently my fake husband. Okay *he's* not really fake, and technically the marriage is real and legal. But we've been man and wife for nearly two years, and I haven't seen him since our ceremony on an Army base in Germany.

It's a marriage of convenience. I thought everything we'd done would be enough to appease my grandmother and my cousin so that my grandmother's will wouldn't be contested. But here we are. Grandma isn't even dead yet and Cousin Rick—of the spray tans and questionable business investments—is already stirring the pot of doubts about my "marriage."

It made sense that Flynn and I lived separately when he was on active duty and stationed abroad. Now that he's not? Questions have been raised. I had simply answered that Flynn had wanted to get settled in and make everything ready for me.

Which is why I am now on my way to visit my husband. To Flynn's new address in his new town. A small, adorable town from everything I've seen so far. Saddle Creek, Texas. I mean how cute is that?

"Piglet, are you seeing this sweet little town? A Public library and a lovely park next to the courthouse. Ice cream shoppe, a diner, an old-fashioned mercantile. Can you even stand it?" I ask my dog. She's probably napping in her soft-sided pink kennel, but I talk to her nonetheless. "This is the kind of town I've always wanted to live in. So charming."

I follow the directions my phone map is reading through my car speakers. It leads me a few roads from downtown, but still in what I'd call the hub of the little town. There's nothing sleepy about Saddle Creek. There are people everywhere, and all of the businesses I've passed seem busy.

Whatever brought Flynn here, it feels like a

great place to make a home. Far better than the smoggy swamp that is Houston, where we both grew up.

It's easy enough to find the little row of cabins that are available for rent. I find lucky number seven and park. It takes a bit of work to maneuver my pink monogrammed luggage out of my tiny backseat, but eventually I do it. I try to be subtle about glancing around me, but it's no use. No matter how nonchalant I attempt to be, I still manage to stick out no matter where I am. In this case though, maybe it's a good thing. I know that my snake of a cousin has had some of his goons following me.

Which is part of the reason I'm here in Saddle Creek, to, uh... claim my husband.

In a manner of speaking.

I drag my wheeled bag behind me as I follow the steps that lead up to the cabin. I think my hands are shaking and I'm likely on the verge of nervous giggles. But I'm here. Again, I try to sneak a look over my shoulder. There is another car that's pulled into park and a few across the street. I'm probably being paranoid, but my cousin has been known to do crazy things in pursuit of grandma's money.

So, I'm ninety-nine percent sure he's hired someone to follow me and get "proof" that Flynn and I aren't really married. And then he's going to use that "proof" to convince grandma to cut me out of the will.

And yes, I know how that sounds. After all, I'm in a fake, real marriage to secure my part of the inheritance. So, yes, that's crazy in its own way.

But it's not about the money for me. It's never been about the money.

It's about all the things related to the money. It's about what will happen to the family estate, a grand old house in the Big Piney Woods in east Texas—which I know Rick will sell off without a second thought. Then someone will build a strip mall on it full of greedy cash-loan places and low-end nail salons.

It's about our great-uncle Benny's collection of Art Nouveau jewelry.

Those are the things I care about. Yes, they have financial value, but they also have sentimental value. Like the time Benny won that locket in a card game in France or how he was gifted the ring by a Polish industrialist for helping his family escape to England just before

WWII. Rick doesn't care about the stories behind any of these things; he'd auction off everything just to liquidize the cash. But I do care. Family history matters to me. Family matters to me even if I haven't ever really had much of one.

More than any of those tangible things, I don't' want my cousin in charge of Grandma's care when she does reach end of life. I will only move her into a facility if that is her choice. Otherwise, I will take care of her, just like she always took care of me.

Which is why I'm willing to do anything to protect my part of the inheritance. Even if it means making an absolute fool of myself in front of Flynn Harrington, up to and including begging him to do me one more favor. Even though Flynn is my (nearly) life-long secret crush and the swooniest guy I've ever met.

So after knocking on the wooden door, I make a hasty decision.

The door pulls open and I don't even let myself enjoy how damned beautiful he is before I launch myself at him and press my mouth to his.

He freezes at first, but then his hands scoop under my bottom, picking me up so I can wrap myself around him. And then his tongue is in my mouth. He makes some sort of growly noise that is hands-down the sexiest thing I've ever heard.

I had not anticipated this. I thought I'd just give him a hello kiss to let anyone who might be following me get a perfect picture of my wedded bliss. But Flynn is kissing me. Maybe he didn't recognize me. Maybe he just will kiss any woman back if she starts it. Then my brain short circuits and I fall into the kiss.

He shifts us and presses my back against the rough cedar planks of the outside wall. Flynn's tongue is a revelation, and I have no doubt that my panties are now drenched. My nipples harden and I shamelessly rub them against his chest while we kiss.

And then, as if the spell is broken, Flynn sets me down. He grabs my hand and pulls me into the cabin, slamming the door behind me. His fingers are raking through his messy dark hair, and there's a few days' growth shadowing his cheeks and jawline.

His dark brown eyes look at me, and I swear my heart is waving a white flag of surrender. This man. Sigh.

chapter **two**

FLYNN

Goddamn, it's about time this woman was here and in my arms. Temple Thorne, the one woman I have no right wanting, considering she's my kid sister's best friend. Not to mention she's from the better side of the tracks than me.

She's been my one constant thought since I returned stateside several months ago. And yeah, she's my wife, but up until that kiss on my doorstep, I'd been under the assumption this marriage was in name only. But maybe she's been thinking about me the way I've been thinking about her.

Her bluebonnet-blue eyes look up at me. I catalog the rest of her. The smattering of freckles across her cheeks and the bridge of her nose. Her dark, curly hair pulled up into a messy bun on the top of her head. The V-neck of her shirt that accents not only her ample cleavage, but the gold chain with the solitaire diamond pendant that dips just between the tops of her breasts. The expanse of pale creamy skin on display makes my mouth water. I want to kiss her again.

"Thanks for playing along out there," she says.

I register her words, but they don't make sense.

"I don't know how many guys my cousin has following me, but I've seen at least one tailing me since I left Houston."

I nod, but still her meaning is lost on me. But I venture a quick question. "So why are you here, Temple? Are you in some kind of trouble?"

That, at least, would make sense. I'm that guy. The one everyone goes to when they have a problem. Not really sure why that's my role but it's been that way for as long as I can remember. Even the other guys on my team come to me for help. I don't even mind. It means I'm useful. That I matter.

"Trouble?" she echoes, then tilts her head. "I guess you could call it trouble." She inhales slowly. "My cousin is contesting the legitimacy of our marriage, and we need to make everything look as real as possible. So I need to live with you, and you need to come home with me this weekend for Grandmother's birthday party." She gives me a forced smile. "Please."

The only thing I hear for certain is that she has not, in fact, been thinking about me the way I've been thinking about her. Of course not. I am her husband for a very specific reason, and desire and affection are not on that list.

I glance at my watch, relieved to see the reminder that I am scheduled to meet up with the guys in fifteen minutes.

"We're going to have to discuss this later. I have a meeting I need to get to." I point at her. "Don't go anywhere until I can properly assess the threat level."

Her big blue eyes widen, but she nods.

I've met her cousin before. He seemed harmless enough at the time. Nothing but a kiss ass and spineless pussy. Didn't mean he couldn't pay other people to do things to Temple. That was something I simply wouldn't allow.

"But you'll be back?" she asks.

"Yeah. Meeting shouldn't take too long." I glance around the small cabin. "Just, uh, make yourself at home."

"Oh, I almost forgot." She reaches into her bra—yeah, you heard that right—and pulls something out. Then she holds her palm out to me. "Here." She holds up the ring.

"What the hell am I supposed to do with that?"

"Wear it. You are my husband."

My cock jerks at her words. Traitorous fucker.

I grab the ring and slide it on my left ring finger. Then look down. "This a woman's ring," I ask, noting the diamond deep set into the silver metal.

"No, it is very much a man's ring. Art Nouveau. It's a family heirloom," she explains. "Will you wear it? For me? At least for now. We can buy you something you like better later."

One hit of those bright blue eyes and I know I've lost the battle.

Awesome.

Hopefully the guys wouldn't notice.

"Of course I'll wear it." I grab my keys and glasses off the small coffee table. "I meant what I said, Temple, stay put."

She gives me a nod, then I turn and leave before I do something really stupid. Like kiss her again.

Maybe I shouldn't be leaving her alone when she just showed up, but I need some time to wrap my brain around everything that happened in the past ten minutes. Besides, I really do have a meeting I have to attend for work.

Ten minutes later, I pull up outside the new VFW hall out on the loop. I never saw the old hall, since this new one was already up and running by the time I moved here two months ago. I have no idea if this post is nicer than most —though I suspect it is—because I never joined a VFW while I was still serving.

I know from what Dane has told me that the rebuild of this post was funded by donations collected during the annual Bluebonnet Festival. Which might seem silly, but based on the number of tourists I've seen in town since bluebonnets started popping up along the highway, I'm guessing it's a pretty big tourist draw.

The hall is a nice mix of functional and clean. It's not fancy, but it's well-lit and smoke-free. I wave at a table of old-timers playing poker and at the cluster of guys playing darts towards the back before making my way to the canteen to order a beer.

Yeah, I know it sounds suspicious. A "work meeting" at the VFW hall over beers at six-thirty on a weeknight? If I was married (to a wife I lived with), it would sound like nothing more than an excuse to get out of the house.

But when I left active service, I took a job working for Great Dane's Dog Sanctuary, a non-profit focused on rescuing shelter dogs from around Texas. Everyone who works for Great Dane's is former military.

When my buddy Dane Whitmore first started it about a year ago, he never imagined how quickly it would grow. He just wanted a place for dogs no one wanted and retired soldiers who didn't know what to do next. It started with a couple hundred acres and thirty-five dogs. Then Dane fell in love with his wife Shelby. She started doing social media for the sanctuary in her spare time. Some videos went viral, and donations and grants started rolling in.

Now, Great Danes employs seven of us. I was brought on to help with construction of the new buildings, since I served in the Army Corps of Engineers. All the guys at tonight's meeting help with some aspect of running the sanctuary.

We started holding "board meetings" here for two reasons: first off, we all like supporting the local post and, secondly, now that Dane is a bit of an internet celebrity, it's nice to meet some place out of the way where he won't be recognized by "fans."

By the time I get there, the guys are already there and shooting the shit. These meetings are partly for work, since during the workday, we're all scattered all over the sanctuary getting shit done, and partly social. I've only just settled into my chair at the table when I catch Beau, our class clown, giving me the side-eye.

"Seriously, is no one else going to ask?" Beau asks.

No one responds, which frankly isn't all that unusual when it comes to Beau's outbursts. We can never guess what he's thinking; his ADHD makes it nearly impossible to follow his train of thought.

“Fine,” Beau says. “I’ll do it. Hey Flynn.”

Oh shit.

“What’s with the big diamond ring on your finger?”

The rest of the guys’ eyes lock on me.

Liam’s brows raise. “Care to share with the class?”

I rub at the back of my neck. “So, I’m married,” I say. As if those three words explain everything.

“What?” Dane asks. “Since when?”

“Almost two years, actually.”

“Paperwork, exchanging of vows, all of that?” Beau asks.

Evan stares at me. “Did you forget to mention it or were you just not planning to tell us?”

“Yes, it’s legal. No, I didn’t forget to tell you. I just didn’t think it would matter once I got stateside,” I say.

“Two fucking years,” Cruz says. “You’re going to have to back up and explain this.”

“Did she leave you or something? Hook up

with another guy while you were gone?" Jack asks.

Everyone knows how his ex did him dirty while he was on duty. Thankfully he found Lucy when he moved here and now he's engaged. I've never seen the guy happier.

"It's a legal marriage, but not really a real marriage," I say. "A marriage of convenience for her to secure her inheritance."

"How long do you have to pretend? Two years seems long enough for an inheritance to go through probate court and anything else," Liam says.

"Inheritance hasn't happened yet. Grandmother is still alive." I pinch the bridge of my nose. "It's complicated. The whole Thorne family is complicated. In any case, we thought the union itself would be enough but evidently her cousin is questioning the legitimacy of our marriage and causing all kinds of problems."

"What are you going to do?" Cruz asks.

"She showed up at my cabin right before I came here. Said we need to live together for the time being and make things look real."

Beau makes a woo-hoo noise. "So your fake wife just strolled back into town and wants to play house? Buddy, this is better than anything on reality television."

"Thanks for the support, Beau," I deadpan.

"I still don't understand why you didn't tell us," Evan says. "We're family. Even if it wasn't going to be real when you got home. Two damn years, Flynn."

Evan is the youngest of us and the most sensitive. Comes with being a medic. He's got a big heart.

"I'm sorry, kid. I wasn't trying to leave you out. I just didn't think it was going to impact anything."

"And instead, it looks like it's impacting everything," Liam says. "What do you know about the level of threat from the cousin?"

"I've met him. He's not the kind to get his own hands dirty. He'd definitely pay someone else to do that. Temple said she thought someone had been following her from Houston," I say.

"And you left her alone in your cabin?" Cruz asks. "Is that wise?"

"Maybe not, but I think anyone following her now is just doing recon. I don't think her cousin is dangerous, just a greedy motherfucker."

"How much of an inheritance are we talking about?" Dane asks.

"Honestly, I don't even know. It's a lot. They're one of the oldest prominent families in Houston society. Several zeroes is what I'm guessing."

"Pretending to be in love with a hot chick shouldn't be a problem, even for you," Beau says. "But if you need some pointers, I'm always here."

I flip him the bird. "Wait, I never said she was hot."

"I'm just guessing you wouldn't have married her if you thought she was a troll," Beau says with a shrug.

"She's my kid sister's best friend," I say, as way of explaining.

"I think what you're not saying says plenty," Liam says.

"Exactly," Cruz says. "You're obviously attracted to her."

I do not deny nor confirm.

"A few public kisses and embraces should be enough to prove to her cousin that y'all are the real deal," Beau says.

I didn't know if I could survive any more of

Temple's kisses. It would only make me want a lot more than she was willing to give.

Cruz stands. "I'm going to go to your cabin with you to help you do a threat analysis. The sooner we know about what this cousin is up to, the better."

If anyone was going to do it, Cruz was the best choice. He would also give me the least amount of shit about Temple. At least, I think.

So we leave the hall and make our way—thankfully it's a short drive—to the row of cabins.

We both scan our surroundings as we walk up to my front door.

"Nondescript sedan parked across the street in front of the elementary school," Cruz says.

"Yeah, I saw him. That fucker better not have someone tailing her."

We step into my living room, and at first I think maybe I opened the wrong cabin. There's so much color everywhere it looks like a bag of Skittles exploded in here. Bright pieces of clothing drape over nearly every piece of furniture and there are decorative pillows tossed onto the sofa. Pieces of pink luxury luggage sit like frosted little soldiers guarding the space.

But then I see the red silk hammock-like thing hanging from the main center beam in my living room. Temple is there, somehow entwined in the fabric, upside down in what might be an inverted warrior pose.

"So either Cirque du Soleil is training in your house, or should I just assume that's the little missus?" Cruz says.

Temple moves to another position, seemingly unaware of our intrusion. Then she does a spin and lands on her feet. She smiles broadly, then walks towards us… wearing nothing but skintight leggings and a sports bra.

Fuck my life.

"I'm Cruz," my buddy says, holding his hand out.

"Oh, is this one of your friends?" Temple asks me.

I nod, still unable to put anything into words. The urge to cover her body so Cruz can't see every one of her thick curves is so strong I have to clench my hands into fists.

Then suddenly there's yipping at my feet. I look down to find some sort of dog. At least I think it's a dog, from the noises it's making. But the large bat-like ears make it look comical. As does the little hop his body makes with every yip.

She scoops him up. "Piglet, you are a terrible guard dog. They could have already murdered me, and you're just now letting me know they're here. Silly boy." She ruffles the thin wispy hairs between his ears. He gives her another yip, then his tongue lolls out to the side.

"Why don't you go check into our friend down the street," Cruz says. "I'll keep an eye on your wife."

I nod.

Cruz follows me to the door. "She's trouble."

"She's temporary," I say.

"Obviously. Why else would you look like you swallowed your tongue when she untangled herself from all that silk?"

"Shut up."

Cruz just chuckles as I walk out the front door.

chapter three

TEMPLE

The guys have left me inside, alone again. Presumably they're outside talking about me. That's what people do. Though they did say they were checking on a suspicious car.

Flynn's cabin is feeling like home, oddly enough. Strange even for me, who can carve out a space for myself in nearly any environment. He didn't even blink at the way I'd scattered my clothes and pillows. The pillows so it looks like I live here–the clothes because I couldn't find my favorite sports bra when I was feeling antsy and needed to do some yoga to calm myself down.

Okay, that's a lie, he totally blinked. Several times, if I'm honest. His thickly lashed brown eyes had surveyed the room, scanning back and forth. But he hadn't said a word. Even when Piglet made himself known.

My partner in crime is currently snoring next to me on the couch. After Cruz left to join Flynn outside, I grabbed my laptop to check email and —what else, I'm not sure. I just needed to do something with my hands.

I could have gotten back up in my yoga hammock, but judging by Flynn's face when he saw me up there, I decided to wait. Maybe he just needs to be assured that it's perfectly safe. I am a professional Yogi.

The door opens and Flynn strolls back into the small cabin. I set my laptop on the coffee table and close it.

"Everything okay?" I ask.

"Yes. The car we'd seen earlier was gone and I walked the perimeter of the area and couldn't find anyone."

"Maybe it was just my imagination."

He shakes his head. "You're not the paranoid type."

His words are stated as a fact.

Like he knows me.

I mean we do know each other, but we haven't been around one another in years. He knew me as a teenager, but his statement rings true. I've never been overly suspicious about anything. Except maybe my cousin's moral compass.

I watch him step into the kitchen and grab a glass from a cabinet, then fill it with water at the fridge. He downs the entire thing. Watching his throat work to swallow is mesmerizing and it occurs to me that I'm staring at him.

It's hard not to. He's beautiful. Tall and broad without being overly bulky. Just perfectly honed muscles, initially from high school sports and then the Army. His dark hair is longer than the last time I saw him. Longer on the top and trimmed tightly to his head above his ears.

I want to strip his clothes off him and catalog every scar and tattoo. I know he has some of both. He had stitches on his arm and neck at our wedding ceremony and he mentioned something about some new ink.

Oh, who am I kidding? I want to see him naked because he's so sexy and I want to ride him like a pony.

But that is not what this marriage is about.

"Everything okay, Temple?" he asks.

He caught me staring, so I give him a small smile. "Yeah, just lost in thought, I guess." Thoughts about how amazing your tight ass would look sans jeans and boxers. If he even wears boxers. "What kind of underwear do you wear?" I blurt.

Temple Thorne: excellent at ice breakers. Now available for your next party.

"What?" he asks, a frown creasing his forehead.

"Well, I am your wife." I shrug. "Just seems like something I should know."

He shoves off of the kitchen counter and walks towards me. He's all casual prowling grace. That's a thing, right?

"You going to tell me about your underwear?" he asks.

Ugh, why was that hot? "I don't think there are as many options for women."

"Inaccurate, but we'll move on."

"I'm a no-frills cotton kind of girl," I admit. "Pretty low key and plain."

"Boxer briefs. And I like ones with nerdy

stuff on them." His arms cross over his chest, and I swear he's smirking at me.

"Like protractors and calculators?"

He laughs. "Not exactly. Though I do have some with math equations on them."

"I never knew they had novelty underwear for y'all."

"We've come a long way since tighty-whities."

That makes me laugh because what are we even talking about? I'm so weird sometimes.

He comes over and sits on the coffee table facing me. "Okay, now that we've gotten the awkward underwear conversation out of the way, tell me what's going on."

"Just my cousin being his obnoxious self," I say.

"I need more words, Temple."

I snort. "No one has ever asked *me* for more words."

He taps his knee against mine. "Your grandmother, is she still...?"

His question hangs in the air, but I know what he's asking. "Inexplicably still alive. The doctors have given up trying to give us a timeline anymore. Her body is definitely weaker, but it's her mind that we're losing more rapidly."

That warrants me a knee squeeze from one of his big hands. I bet his hands are big enough that he could legitimately cup my tits.

For fuck's sake, Temple, get your head out of the slutty gutter. Focus.

"In any case, she's having more bad days than good days at this point. I know that Rick and Lotus are conspiring to put her in a memory care facility. But Granny was very specific when she said she wanted to live the rest of her days in her own home. She has twenty-four hour care. She should get to make that decision. It's her damn money."

"Right now you're still listed as executor, right?" he asks.

I blow out a breath. "Technically, no. That is tied up in court because of my cousin. So the family attorney is executor."

"And Rick the dick is calling our marriage into question?" Flynn asks.

"Correct."

"I take it you've shown him the marriage license and all of that?"

"Of course. I think for him it's less about

whether or not the marriage is legal and more about if it's a real marriage," I say. "Honestly, it feels like any moment he's going to call a doctor in to examine me to see if we've been intimate."

Flynn's already dark eyes go black. "Has he threatened that?" his tone is sharp and jagged.

"No. No one does that anymore. And I've clearly read too many medieval romance novels."

Stop talking, Temple. Stop talking, especially about being intimate with Flynn.

I wave my hand as if to wipe away the last few moments.

"Please understand it's not about the money. I truly do not care about her money. But I do care about some of the family heirlooms and what happens to Grandma when the rest of her memory fades. I think Rick preys on her memory issues, planting lies and ramping up her paranoia."

"Hey, I'm not judging you, whatever your motives are. If you were just in it for the money. It's your family inheritance; you deserve at least half of it."

"I know, I just hate for people to think I'm some money hungry loser. I own my own business. I have an income to take care of myself. If

Grandma hadn't created that weird competition in the first place, maybe Rick wouldn't be so angry with me."

"Agreed. Having a race to the alter has strong Hammerstein musical vibes."

That makes me smile. "You were so tolerant of me and Daisy singing showtunes in the backseat of your car."

He gives me a fond smile that just about breaks my heart. He still sees me as a little sister type.

I blow out a breath.

"We'll figure this out," he says.

I nod. Regardless of how he sees me, at least I'm not in this completely alone. "Flynn, I need you to know that, had I known this would stretch beyond that first year, I never would have asked you. I know this is inconvenient, and now I've come here to hijack your life even further."

"You haven't hijacked anything," he says. "Now that I'm retired from the military, I'm starting over."

I snort. "So it's the perfect time to have an inconvenient wife?"

"Something like that."

"I suppose we need some ground rules if we're going to be suddenly living together."

He stares at me blankly for a minute, then nods. "Right. Because we need to live together to make it look as real as possible."

"Exactly." Piglet rolls over on his back, legs in the air, and releases one of his snort-snores. "You're not allergic to dogs, are you?"

"Is that actually a dog?"

I gasp, but I'm still smiling. I put my hands over Piglet's ears. "He can hear you."

"He snores louder than I do."

"Oh, do you snore?"

He shrugs. "Not sure, actually. Guys never mentioned it when we bunked together. Also, no, I'm not allergic to dogs."

This simultaneously feels awkward and comfortable all at the same time. Which frankly is confusing as hell.

Is it the kiss? Should I explain more about why I kissed him?

I should have read up on being a fake wife before coming here.

Though, it's doubtful there are how-to guides out there.

Maybe after this, I'll write one.

chapter four

FLYNN

I'm beginning to wonder if I have more residual damage to my brain than the doctors claimed. A grade two concussion can cause long-lasting problems. Like the inability to stop thinking about my wife's panty choice.

Basic cotton. But what color? Do they have a little bow right above her belly button? Are there small flowers decorating the fabric?

At least she put on a shirt that covers all the exposed skin from her aerial yoga. Seeing every one of her plump curves highlighted with the clinging fabric had blood rushing so quickly to my dick that I got lightheaded.

I've watched her do her yoga before, but never in the same room. I've only ever seen her through my laptop screen on her instructional videos. She's always so damn graceful; her movements languid and seductive. Though I'm likely the only creepy fucker who watches her and thinks that.

She is my wife though. Seems I should have some rights where that's concerned.

"I suppose we will need to have some public displays of affection to make our love look real," she says.

"Like the kiss from earlier," I say.

"Exactly. Sorry about ambushing you like that." She gives me a self-deprecating smile. "In case my cousin did send someone to follow me, I wanted to make our reunion look as real as possible."

"Apology is unnecessary. I get it and I agree, we want this to look as real as we can make it." It will require no faking on my part because fuck if I don't want to lay her down right now and cover her entire body in kisses.

My wife.

When had I started thinking about Temple Thorne like that? Yes, technically we've been married for nearly two years. But while I was finishing up my last tour, my mind was on the mission. Can't afford to be distracted over there.

Once I was stateside, all bets were off. Temple crept into my mind more and more. Even while recuperating from the last big mission that went a little sideways. It's what brought the rest of our team home. Dane and Jack and Liam had already gone by then. So it had been me and Cruz, and Beau and Evan, with some new guys rounding out the team.

"Is there any kind of touching you wouldn't be comfortable with?" Temple asks. "I mean in public, the decent kind or whatever? I'm just going to shut up now."

I want to tell her she can be as indecent with me as she wants in or out of public, but she doesn't see me that way.

"You want to know if I have any hard limits?" I ask.

She nods in lieu of giving me any more of her words. Clearly people are still telling her that she talks too much. I, for one, could never tire of her sweet voice.

"No. I'm new to this town, so I'd rather not get arrested for anything pornographic, but everything else, I'm game for."

Her lips part and she stares at me with her wide blue eyes. Her pink tongue dips out and wets her lips. "I met Mrs. Henderson," she says.

"Who?"

"Uh... your neighbor. The one behind you in cabin fourteen." Temple points somewhere over her shoulder.

"You already met a neighbor?" I've been here for a month and wasn't even aware I had actual neighbors.

"Yes, she was very friendly. And helpful. I needed to know if that top center beam was structurally sound for me to use my hammock on it." Her shoulders lift in a shrug. "She assured me it was and then called me your 'pretty little wife that you've been hiding from the world'. Then she said something about how it must be because of all the baby making we were working on."

I nearly choke on my own spit. Because in that moment all I can think about is Temple swollen and ripe with my kid. What is it about this woman that brings out my inner caveman?

I hadn't even realized I actually had one of those.

"What did you tell her?" I ask.

"I just laughed and told her that she was right, when you have a husband who looks like mine, there's no way you can keep your hands to yourself."

I suppress a groan. She's obviously trying to kill me.

"Apparently some people in Saddle Creek skip straight over the small talk and jump right into bedroom and reproductive talk," Temple says nonchalantly.

She's clearly not thinking about us rolling around in the bed naked, me trying to pump her full of my seed. I needlessly wipe my palms against my denim clad thighs.

"You said something about a party for your grandmother?" I ask.

"Right. You remember how obnoxious my family can be. Houston society meets country club chic." She rolls her eyes.

"Rick the dick?"

"He'll be there, no doubt following us around with a microscope. Then there's his wife, Lotus."

"His wife's name is Lotus?" I ask, scratching at the back of my neck.

"Yes. I don't think that's the name her mama gave her, but as far as I know it's her legal name. She's a real treat, so be excited you get to meet her," Temple says.

"Maybe we should try to get you pregnant. That would end all of the suspicions about our marriage," I say.

Temple's gasp is quiet and had I not been looking at her pretty face, I might have missed it. She looks... panicked, maybe? It's hard to tell.

I wink at her to diffuse the tension.

She releases a small chuckle. "We only need to stay one night. We show up for the party, act like we're stupid in love, and hope Grandma is having one of her more lucid moments so she sees it."

"What exactly does 'stupid in love' look like?" I can't help but ask.

My wife's bluebonnet colored eyes find mine. "Lots of eye contact. Hand holding. Probably some kisses. You might want to use a pet name with me." Again she shrugs. "Real couples do that, don't they?"

I skip answering her question because I

joined the Army right after high school graduation and haven't had any adult relationships other than with her. I haven't touched another woman since Temple and I got married. Despite the fact that this marriage was supposed to be in name only, I honor my vows.

"I'll think of something. Good thing we have the Bluebonnet Festival tomorrow night. We can use that as a dress rehearsal. Make sure we get lots of 'stupid in love' activities played out."

"Oh, a real small-town festival. It'll be like living in one of those charming holiday movies."

"Something like that."

She leans forward and puts her hand on my knee. "Flynn, seriously, thank you for letting me completely tip your life upside down for a little while. I know I owe you. And don't worry, when the time comes and we need to get divorced, I'll make sure I'm the bad guy so you can find you a real wife someday."

With that, she stands and disappears into my bathroom.

I want to call after her to tell her she can't wear only yoga pants and sports bras in the cabin. I won't make it.

Too. Fucking. Tempting.

But I decide to wait. We can always discuss clothing requests later.

I go about making sure my bed is ready for her, then grab some extra bedding and bring it out to the living room.

But her words keep echoing in my ear.

I don't want another wife, real or otherwise. But I can't tell her that. I hate that she's so unsure of herself, that it's so natural for her to assume that I couldn't possibly want her. Temple is one of those people who stands out in a crowd. A supernova in the midst of fading stars.

Maybe through this experience—while I'm her husband—I can show her just how spectacular she is.

chapter **five**

FLYNN

ME: I think I'm in trouble.

CRUZ: Ask me if I'm surprised.

ME: Yeah, yeah. Can you just hit me with some of your wise old man advice?

CRUZ: Ouch. I'm only forty. You act like I'm the crypt keeper over here.

ME: Sorry.

CRUZ: I'm assuming you want to know what to do about the fact that you're in love with your wife.

ME: Whoa. Did not say love.

ME: Do I want to fuck her? Yes. And often.

ME: But love? Seems unlikely.

ME: I knew her growing up because she's Daisy's best friend. But we don't really know one another as adults.

CRUZ: And you want to know her in the Biblical sense. I get it.

ME: I'm bringing her to the festival tomorrow. It's going to be our practice evening of behaving like a real couple before we have to go to her grandmother's birthday party.

CRUZ: Her grandmother who is dying? That one?"

ME: Don't try to make sense of the wealthy elite from Houston. They're a whole different breed of Texan.

CRUZ: So this weekend will be what tells you how to proceed.

ME: Meaning?

CRUZ: Meaning you'll know one way or another if you just want to do the naked hokey pokey with her or if you want to wife her up.

CRUZ: Again.

CRUZ: For real.

CRUZ: Whatever.

chapter six

TEMPLE

My husband is holding my hand as we walk towards the crowds at the county fairgrounds. Piglet is trotting along next to me, his leash, for the most part, unnecessary because he won't willingly leave my side. But I never want to take chances when it comes to my boy.

I'm wearing a brand new, adorable dress that's part sundress, part vintage pin-up girl style. It's got abstract wildflowers drawn all over it and I've gotta say, the halter is doing fabulous things for my boobs. I paired it with a fabulous new pair of cowgirl boots.

"Have I told you how nice you look?" Flynn asks.

"Not in detail," I say with a smile. "I found the cutest store downtown this morning when you went for a run. Got the whole ensemble there.

Frankly, it had been surprising, to say the least, to find a shop in such a small town that stocks cute clothes for plus sized women. The two women who co-own the store, Madison and Jade, are both curvy girls, so that probably explains it. Still, it felt fortunate. I had not packed anything that felt appropriate to wear to a small town, outdoor festival.

"Well, it all looks great on you."

"I wanted to make sure I looked worthy of being your arm candy." I hip check him. Am I flirting with my not-quite-real husband? Maybe. Or maybe I'm fishing for compliments and basking in the glow of whatever attention he gives me.

Having to pretend to be in love—in public—will be no hardship for me. I've crushed on Flynn since I was a girl. And he's only gotten hotter as we've grown up.

Daisy and I had hit it off that summer when we'd met at choir camp. I'd seen glimpses of her older brother from the car window when he'd drop her off and pick her up. Shortly after school had started, they'd had auditions for the school musical. That year we would be doing *Seven Brides for Seven Brothers*. I tried out for all of the matronly parts only to be mortified when the choir director cast me as one of the sisters.

At the time I wasn't the biggest girl in choir, but I was close to it. Far heavier than most of the other fifteen-year-old freshmen. Knowing that some puny high school choir boy was going to have to carry me off stage in a scene made me want to fall into a hole.

It had gotten even worse when I overheard some of the boys in the cast discussing it, almost drawing straws as to who would have to carry the heifer, as they'd called me. But when it came time for the first day of rehearsal, Flynn had shown up as my partner. He'd been the one to carry me that day in practice and every day thereafter.

I heard a rumor he'd asked the choir director for the part, and I asked Flynn about it one day. He'd tilted my chin up to look at him and told me I was perfect just the way I was and not to let anyone ever tell me differently.

My poor teenage heart hadn't stood a chance. Not against Flynn's kindness. He'd been saving me since I was a girl, and I wish I knew one way I could thank him for always being my hero.

"I'll get to meet the rest of your friends tonight, right?" I ask.

"Yeah, they should all be here." His hand squeezes mine. Then he stops walking abruptly. He bends and scoops Piglet up. Flynn nods to the swollen crowds of people ahead of us. "Don't want him to get trampled."

Why does that make me want to cry? Probably because it's a show of real affection. Even if that affection is for my dog. It's been just me and Piglet against the world for a while now. Especially since Daisy moved overseas.

Flynn's gaze searches my face. He frowns. "Are you okay?"

I nod. "Just missing your sister like a sentimental fool."

He nods. "Seems like it's past time for her to come home."

"Maybe when she does, she'll join us here in

Saddle Creek. I am already in love with this town."

We walk under the banner that reads: *Saddle Creek's Forty-seventh Annual Bluebonnet Festival.*

There are a variety of tents along the far side and one large one with a raised stage. A band is playing. Country music, of course. And there's a make-shift dance floor in front of that. Looks like it's made of plywood covered in either sawdust or cornmeal. Only a few old-timers and little kids are dancing at the moment.

I do my best to not focus on how right Flynn's big fingers threaded through mine feels. He looks good enough to eat, with his worn-in jeans and scuffed boots. The black t-shirt brandishing a logo on the back for Great Dane's Dog Sanctuary molds to his broad shoulders.

It's on my tongue to ask him about it, when "Yo! Harrington!" rings through the crowd.

"For fuck's sake," Flynn mutters under his breath.

The guy comes forward, backwards ball cap covering his dark blond hair. He's a little shorter than Flynn, but stockier. When he sees me, his handsome face splits into a huge smile.

"This the old ball and chain?" He gives me

a wicked grin and a wink. "I'm Beau. Flynn's hot friend. I gotta say, when we found out he was married, we kinda thought he made you up."

That makes me laugh and I'm instantly charmed. I can already tell that Beau is one of those people that you meet and feel like you've known them your entire life.

"Temple, this is Beau, the crazy one of the group. Beau, this is my wife, Temple."

My wife, Temple.

I think that made my panties a little damp. Which is weird. Could also be caused by Flynn dropping my hand and wrapping an arm around my waist, pulling me close to him.

I hold my hand out to Beau. "I can assure you, I am the very real and not at all made-up wife."

"I can see that, darlin'" Beau says.

"Fuck off, Beau. Go find your own wife."

Beau just laughs good-naturedly. "Come on you two love birds. The rest of the team is over by the beer tent."

"Of course they are," Flynn says. He leans close to my ear. "Do you drink? Seems like something I should know."

"On occasion. Though beer is not my favorite."

"We'll find you something else."

"Shelby's drinking a hard lemonade," Beau says as we walk towards a group of guys. "Homemade too. Smells amazing."

Flynn's eyes cut to mine. "Want one of those?"

"Sure."

"Dude," Beau says. "Did you know you have some sort of furry creature growing out from under your arm?"

Flynn nods. "That's Piglet."

"That is not a pig," Beau says.

"He's a dog," I say.

Beau looks at me, his gaze unbelieving. "You sure about that?"

I laugh. "I am. I even had his DNA tested. He's mostly Papillon, but he's got a bit of Corgi, Chihuahua and Maltese mixed in there."

Beau makes a huh noise. "Cute," he says dryly.

I reach over and cover Piglet's ears. "Don't you listen to him, baby. Mama thinks you're beautiful. Yes, she does. And I think Daddy does too."

I'm just playing a part. Being silly. But my words slam into me with all the unintended meanings. It's then that I notice my boobs are pressed right up on Flynn's other arm. I might as well be climbing the man.

"Daddy," Beau repeats with a snort.

I pull away from my not-quite-real-husband and then we're enveloped by the crowd. His Army buddies and spouses, I assume.

Cruz nods from one of the seats around the picnic table the group has commandeered.

"Hey Temple," he says with a friendly nod.

"Hi again, Cruz."

Then there are two women making their way through the group of guys.

"I'm Shelby, Dane's wife." She points over her shoulder and a big, broad and thick cowboy raises his beer bottle in my direction.

"And I'm Lucy. I belong to that behemoth over there. Jack!" she calls out.

Jack—I'm assuming—looks up and smiles at her. "You need something, Pocket?"

"Nope," she says, hitting that P hard. "Just showing off your pretty face."

He is, in fact, very attractive and big. In fact, all of the guys seem to be. Flynn introduces the rest of the guys. There's the babyfaced Evan, whom they all seem to call 'kid' or 'doc', and Liam who greets me politely, then goes back to leaning against the table, eyes dark and brooding. And just like that I've met them all.

Flynn hands me Piglet and I do another round of introductions while my husband walks off to grab us drinks.

"We're so glad to have another wife in the group," Shelby says. "Lucy and I have known each other forever. So it's really nice to have someone new."

"I hope you're causing Flynn all kinds of trouble," Lucy says with a grin.

"I'm pretty sure he thinks I'm a handful," I admit.

"I have big hands, I can manage," Flynn says from behind me. One of said big hands lands on my hip and squeezes. "Here you go, Angel." He holds out a plastic cup filled with ice and lemonade.

"Thank you," I say.

He's all nonchalant like he didn't just call me 'Angel' or squeeze my hip or admit he has big enough hands for me. If we were in a Regency novel, I would be swooning right now. Instead, we're at a ridiculously charming small-town festival with friendly people who seem legitimately glad to meet me. And my hot as fuck husband is manhandling my hips.

I don't know if I'm going to survive the evening with my practical cotton panties intact.

chapter seven

FLYNN

I haven't let my wife out of my sight very often tonight. She's meshing really well with the other two wives. And she's handled the guys' teasing with humor and grace.

Fuckers.

The sun has begun to set and it's showcasing all the twinkle lights put out around the fairgrounds. I'm man enough to admit that it's definitely romantic out here. The dance floor has progressively gotten fuller as the bands have become better and better.

"Are you serious with this right now?" Temple asks.

Shelby laughs.

I glance up at the stage, but my wife's surprise is lost on me. "Who is it?" I ask.

"None other than pop princess, Jess Munoz," Temple says enthusiastically. "She lives here!"

"My sister-in-law," Shelby says. "She's married to Dane's older brother, Grady. She is so down to Earth and amazing." Shelby nods to the stage. "In a minute, another of our locals and one of her friends will get up there with her."

"Who?" Temple asks, practically bouncing on the picnic bench next to me.

"Micah Stone."

Temple playfully swats Shelby's arm "You are lying."

Shelby just shakes her head.

"Angel," I say, getting to my feet. "Pass Piglet to someone and let's go dance."

"You don't have to ask me twice," she says.

Shelby happily takes the dog from Temple and I thread our fingers together to pull her out to the dance floor. Once my boots hit the harder surface, I pull her into my arms. I've got one hand splayed across her back and I'm holding her hand with my other. And I push her backwards into a classic Texas two-step.

She beams up at me. "I didn't know you could dance."

"You wound me," I say. "Surely you haven't forgotten all of our amazing dancing from the play?"

"Ah, yes, the first time you played my husband," she says. "I remember all of it. But it was choreographed; I was so awkward."

"You could not have been more awkward than me learning to dance in P.E. classes."

She laughs. "Pretty sure they don't let you leave high school in Texas without learning how to two-step."

"Don't forget the square dancing," I say.

"How could I ever forget the Do-si-do?"

We dance in silence for a few measures before she speaks again. "I'd really love to know how to repay you for all the times you've saved me."

"Unnecessary. I get the benefit of your company."

"If you ever think of something though, promise you'll tell me what it is?"

"Yeah, Angel, I promise."

From this close, I can smell the citrusy scent of her shampoo. Not to mention I've got a spectacular view of her cleavage.

We dance well together, and I never considered myself a great dancer, so I'm guessing it has more to do with her skills than mine.

"So you and the guys are all wearing matching shirts. What's up with that?" she asks.

"After I got released from the military hospital and then finished up my time working a desk, I came here. We all did. Liam got out a while back and had started a dog sanctuary. But he ran into some land problems with his ex and had to send the dogs here to Dane."

"Ohhhh, thus Great Dane's Dog Sanctuary. Clever."

"Yes. I didn't have anything to do with that cleverness."

"So your whole team or unit or whatever moved here to run the sanctuary together?"

I nod. "Something like that. There are a couple of guys still on active duty, but this is the majority of us. And these are the guys I worked with the longest."

"What all does the sanctuary do?" she asks.

"Right now we house more than eighty dogs.

Dane has a huge piece of property. I've been working mostly with Jack to get structures built. But I've also been working on a program to help train the dogs for different services."

"That's amazing," she says.

I swear, as she gazes up at me, I see pride shining in her eyes. So I do the only thing I can think of; I dip my head and move my mouth over hers. She's so responsive as her lips part immediately. I take the opportunity and slide my tongue against hers. Her arms come up and around my neck, and I grip her hips as the fronts of our bodies fuse together.

I'm pretty sure we've stopped dancing at this point, and I'm just full-on making out with my wife. In public. Not my usual style, but I'm taking advantage of the environment.

Finally, I pull back and press my forehead to hers. We're both breathing a little heavier.

"Did you see someone suspicious?" she whispers.

"What?"

"Like whoever my cousin might have hired?"

I shake my head. "Not exactly."

"I have to admit," she says. "When you kiss me like that, you make me almost forget this is pretend." She chuckles. "So, I guess, well done, soldier."

I give her bottom a playful swat as I lead her off the dance floor. "You never know who's watching," I say.

chapter **eight**

TEMPLE

By the time we make it back to Flynn's cabin, I'm a soaked mess. Well, my panties are, at least. I make a beeline for the bathroom, so damn thankful I thought to bring my little bullet with me.

Being in public with Flynn is dangerous to my libido. It's actually kind of a miracle I didn't try to hump his leg at the picnic table. After our dance, his friends had teased us mercilessly about our passionate display on the dance floor. Flynn had just shrugged and told them to stop being jealous and to get their own damn wives.

I'm so turned on right now, I don't think it will take long for me to explode. I pull off my dress, thankful I left my boots by the front door. I turn the shower on and remove the rest of my under garments. Then I'm stepping under the heat of the water. My nipples tighten to needy little beads, and I turn to face the shower streams to let it sluice down my body.

I turn on the bullet and nestle it against my clit. I moan as the immediate buzzing spreads pleasure through my body. This is not my first time masturbating with Flynn on my mind. He's always been my favorite fantasy.

Now, though, I know what he tastes like. What his hands feel like on my body. At least certain parts. I'm pretty sure Flynn is an ass man, judging by how many times he touched mine tonight.

I turn the level up one on my vibe and tilt my head back against the shower wall. It doesn't take long before I'm coming, my pussy squeezing against nothing as the climax shudders through me.

Hopefully, that'll take the edge off. I set the bullet down on the built-in soap shelf and go about finishing my shower. It's not until half an hour later, when I'm snuggled beneath sheets that smell like Flynn, that I realize I left my toy in the shower.

"Shit!" I hiss. I tiptoe out of bed and peek into the hall. Sure enough, the bathroom door is closed, and I can hear the shower running.

Awesome.

Now my husband knows exactly what I was doing in there. Well, that won't be awkward tomorrow on our drive to Houston.

I squeeze my eyes shut and pad back to Flynn's bedroom. It could've been worse. He could've walked in on me mid orgasm.

chapter nine

FLYNN

My wife got herself off in my shower last night.

That has been my primary thought since I stepped into the shower after she'd gone to bed. When I'd found her little vibrator sitting on my soap dish, my half chub had gone to full erection in a single breath. I'd no sooner seen the small hot pink vibe than I'd fisted my cock. It hadn't taken me long to be spraying cum all over the shower floor, swallowing Temple's name.

I'd decided, then and there, that I was going to do whatever it took to convince Temple to give us a chance. We were good together. Judging from our kisses, we will set the bed on fire when I finally claim her. And now I know for sure that she isn't unaffected by me. She wants me too.

Maybe it'll piss my sister off if I'm married—for real—to her best friend, but at this point, I'm too far gone to give a shit. If I'm not already in love with Temple, it's only a matter of time before I am.

Our drive to Houston has been relatively drama free, which is saying something considering interstate traffic in Texas is always congested. We've kept ourselves occupied by discussing the dog sanctuary and playing "name that tune the fastest" on the oldies station. She's totally beating me, but only because I'm more focused on her than I am on the songs.

Neither one of us can actually sing. Our kids will likely be tone-deaf, but they'll probably be smart.

Our kids. Yeah, I may have already wifed her up, but I'm definitely keeping Temple.

Now, as I maneuver my truck up the wide circular driveway of her family's sprawling estate, I'm more than ready to prove to her stupid cousin that I'm here to stay.

"We're here," Temple says as I put the truck in park.

"We are. You okay?"

"Yeah. Just always a little unsure of how things will be with Grandma on any given day. I get updates during the day from her caregivers, but I still feel guilty I'm not doing more."

"Did you get a nursing degree when I wasn't looking?" I ask. I lean towards her and grip the back of her neck, giving her a squeeze. "You are doing everything right. It's because of you she's still here in her home, correct?"

"Yes. Rick suggested moving her into a care facility even before her memory got really bad."

"Exactly." I search her pretty face, those big guileless eyes of hers. "We've got this." I close the distance between us and give her a quick kiss.

chapter **ten**

TEMPLE

My husband has my vibrator.

Which means he totally knows that I got myself off in his shower last night. And he must know that I know that he knows. But he hasn't said anything about it. After we got to my grandmother's house, we'd both been whisked off to separate activities. As was the way with the country club elite; men go here and women go there. Always reminds me of *Gilmore Girls* reruns with Emily and Richard's posh life.

I've been brought to a salon where they've primped and polished me until I shine. Well, at least they'd done my nails—fingers and toes—given me a facial and had me try on a variety of options for tomorrow's party. I refused to let them color my hair. I happen to like my basic brown, as the stylist called it. I did relent and agree to an un-tinted finishing gloss to add shine. So I'm currently sitting under one of the dryers while the gloss sets.

I know Lotus is here, I've caught glimpses of her long, glossy dark hair in a few of the mirrors.

I know that part of Flynn's day is including some of the same. Possibly a haircut and shave, but definitely a fitting for a suit to wear to the festivities.

It's weird that I'm missing him. We've only been together, in our charade of a marriage, for a couple of days, but I find I'm already accustomed to hearing his deep voice, smelling his scent near me, feeling his hand at the small of my back, or tangled with mine.

My phone vibrates from my lap.

FLYNN: <picture of pink bullet vibrator>

. . .

My cheeks heat and I quickly glance around to make sure no one saw the image. I'm about to type out a response—though I have no idea what I'm going to say—when his next message comes through.

FLYNN: Next time I get to watch.

He wants to watch me? Does that mean I get to watch him? Because sign me up for that peep show.

FLYNN: Seeing that in my shower was an instant turn on.

FLYNN: I'd already been keyed up from having you in my arms all night. The taste of your kiss still lingering in my mouth.

FLYNN: Tell me that's why you needed to get yourself off.

FLYNN: Tell me it's because you want me.

ME: Yes.

ME: Your kiss drove me wild.

ME: It was all about you.

FLYNN: Did you get yourself off?

ME: Yes. Fast and hard.

FLYNN: Me too, Angel.

FLYNN: Fuck, I'm getting hard again just thinking about it.

FLYNN: How much longer are you at that goddamn salon?

ME: Shouldn't be too much longer.

ME: Are you back at the house?

FLYNN: Almost.

FLYNN: In the back of the town car while your douche-wagon of a cousin regales me with his most recent investment success.

ME: Don't believe anything he says.

FLYNN: I'm not even listening. I'm thinking about your sweet, wet <cat emoji>.

My husband is legit sexting me. I'm not even sure what to do with myself, other than to cross my legs and squeeze my thighs together to try and alleviate some of the pressure.

FLYNN: Are you going to let me touch you?

ME: Yes.

FLYNN: Thank fuck. Now get your sweet ass home.

chapter **eleven**

TEMPLE

By the time I make it back to my grandmother's house, it's dark outside and my panties are ruined. My nerves were pretty well shot by the time I climbed into the back of the limousine. So I'd helped myself to a glass of champagne for the drive back to the house.

That alcohol had taken the edge off so I wasn't the sick kind of nervous. No one wants a nervous tummy before sexy times.

That's what was about to happen, right? I mean that's what he'd more or less implied in his texts.

When the sleek black car pulled up into the circular drive, I saw a lone figure leaning against one of the big white columns that flanked the double front doors. As soon as the car is parked, Flynn shoves off the column and opens my car door.

"Wife," he says, holding his hand out to me.

I let him help me out of the car and immediately his hand falls to cup my ass. "Upstairs. Now." His tone is deep and demanding and my nipples pebble in response.

"Are we going to have sex?" I whisper.

"Yes. A lot of it."

That makes me giggle.

We climb the stairs in silence, then he's pulling me towards a room.

"Is this the one they put us in?" I ask, curious that they didn't just give us my room from when I lived here full-time. "Because my old room—"

Flynn's lips crash down onto mine as he closes the bedroom door behind us. He doesn't seem to care about what I was trying to say because he's crowding me into the room.

"Fuck, Temple, I've never been this hard in my whole goddamn life. And in full honesty, I had to take the edge off once already so I didn't come at the first sight of your tits." His voice is ragged as if he is suffering a bit.

Then he's kissing me again and backing me into the room until my legs hit a mattress. His mouth licks down the column of my throat and I slide my hands under the soft cotton of his t-shirt. Warm, hard skin meets my palms, and he groans at my touch.

"To answer the question I think you were asking, I moved us to this room because I wanted some privacy. While I want to prove to Rick the Dick that our marriage is very much real, I don't want to do that by letting him hear you scream my name." He cups my face and leans back a little to meet my gaze. "This is for us. It's not for show. It's not to prove anything."

I swallow hard and nod.

I want to ask what this means for after Houston. If our marriage is real and legal so we get to have sex, but then we will also be getting divorced? Is that what he means?

But, I realize it doesn't actually matter what he means. I'm going to let him fuck me either way. I can't tell him with my words how I feel about him—how I've always felt about him—but I can show him with my body.

I pull his t-shirt off, then run my hands over the muscular ridges of his torso. He's got scars and a couple of tattoos, but mostly it's just skin covered sinew with a dark smattering of hair. I want to touch him everywhere.

"You said you took the edge off already," I say as he continues to trail wet, open-mouthed kisses along my collarbone.

He hums in response. Then his hands are lifting my shirt, dragging it up and off my body. His dark eyes latch onto my bra-covered boobs. It's a pretty bra as far as work-horse bras go. When you have boobs the size of mine, you've gotta go with function over aesthetic. Still, the cream-colored silk and lace do their job, holding my big girls in place, while also being nice to look at.

"Temple," he groans my name, then leans forward and nips at the rise of my left breast. "You have no idea how long I've wanted to see these." His palms come up and cup me, weighing, squeezing.

I reach behind me to unhook it—three prongs for this utilitarian brazier. Then I let the cups loosen and the straps slide down my shoulders.

"What were you thinking about earlier? When you touched yourself?" I ask.

He stands to his full height and lifts his gaze from my boobs to my face. "Truthfully?"

I wince. "Yes." I steel myself, waiting for him to admit he was fantasizing about another woman.

"Eating your kitty."

I gasp.

"It's all I've been able to think about since I found your vibrator. Me licking and sucking at your sweetness until you come all over my face."

I wheeze. Yep, I'm making all the sexy noises, and he's barely touched me.

"You going to let me do that, wife? Can I eat your pussy until you're screaming my name?"

"That feels like a trick question," I manage to say. "I mean, yes, please."

His dark chuckle scatters goosebumps all over my body. My nipples tighten to painful tips.

His thumbs brush over them. "I want to fuck these too. But not now. We'll save that for later." He steps away from me then, pulling off his jeans and kicking them to the side. He's left in a pair of tight boxer briefs, R2D2 style. The bulge is obscene, it's so large.

"Nerdy boxers," I say.

He hums again. "Take off your clothes, Temple." He sits on the floor, leaning his back against the foot of the bed.

I swallow thickly but do as he says. I remove each piece knowing that there's no going back for me after this. I'm giving him every part of me, and I know there will never be another man for me. I feign confidence I don't exactly feel, planting my fists on my hips and looking at his face.

I've got bumps and rolls and dimples and stretch marks, and everything else society tells me isn't sexually attractive. But I can see the lust on my husband's face. He wants me. Maybe not even in spite of my flaws, but because of them. He's always told me I'm perfect just the way I am.

My body isn't perfect, but it's strong and healthy and I'm going to give it all to Flynn Harrington.

chapter
twelve

FLYNN

"You're a fucking goddess," I tell her when she's standing bare in front of me. "Come here, I think this will put me at the perfect height."

She's a little hesitant with her movement forward, but soon she's standing close enough I can smell her arousal. She's not shaved bare, but the dark patch of hair on her mound is trimmed. It wouldn't have mattered to me one way or another, because this is my Temple.

"Put one foot on the bed behind me. I want you opened to me."

She puts her left leg up, which opens her pussy right at my face.

"Perfect," I breathe. "Fuck, you smell good, Angel."

Her fingertips settle on top of my head while I wrap my arms around her body and get my first taste. She's salty and sweet and my dick thumps in my boxers.

I go to work, devouring her with my lips and tongue.

Her little noises of pleasure are addicting, and I just want more and more of them. I squeeze her ass, while my mouth does all the work.

"Flynn," she pants my name. Then she rocks slightly, pressing her pussy to my mouth. "Oh God. It's too much, I can't..."

I hold her body in place, keeping her spread open so I can lick her through it. Right now she's feeling like it's all too sensitive, but I know that just means she's getting really close. I suck her needy little bundle of nerves into my mouth, and she goes off like a goddamn rocket.

Her body pulses against my mouth. Her voice breaks as she cries out my name. Then she all but collapses on my lap.

I hold her to me while her body comes down from its high. She nuzzles against my neck. "You're absurdly good at that," she murmurs into my flesh.

I laugh. "Oh yeah? Maybe you should get me a bumper sticker or a t-shirt."

"I think I want to keep that secret to myself. I don't want a line of women following you around."

I reach between her legs, cupping her mound. "This is the only pussy I want."

"It's all yours."

I stand and pull her onto the bed with me. Immediately her hand slips inside the front of my boxers, gripping my erection.

"Fuck, Angel. Your touch feels so good."

"I don't want anything between us, Flynn. Just you and me. I can pull up my medical records on my phone if you want. But I only ever had one short-lived relationship in college where I was intimate with a guy. It's been years."

"I haven't touched another woman since sometime before we got married," I say.

She looks up at me, her eyes searching my face. "Really?"

"You're my wife. I would never cheat on you."

She pulls me down for a heated kiss and I know she can taste herself on my tongue. "Make me your wife in every way, Flynn, please."

I pull off my boxers and fling them off the bed, then position myself between her thick thighs. She parts for me, her eyes trained on our bodies.

I drag myself against her pussy, lubricating my shaft with her release. Already, she's impossibly hot and wet.

"My wife," I say, then I surge forward, sliding myself home.

She sucks in a breath, her nails digging into my shoulders.

"Too much?" I ask.

"No. You're just not small."

"And you're so damn tight, Angel. I hope I can last; make this good for you."

Her thighs widen, her knees coming up as she wraps her legs around me. "It's already good."

I kiss her as I start to move. The first slide nearly out and then back in makes me clench my teeth.

"Tell me it feels good for you. I gotta move more, Temple. It's too damn good."

"Yes, do it. Fuck me, Flynn."

She doesn't have to tell me twice. I pound into her. The room fills with the sloppy, wet noises of sex.

"Oh my... damn," Temple says.

I shift our position so I'm up on my knees and her ass is tilted up, resting against my thighs. Then I slam down into her from a slightly different angle. This allows me to put my thumb next to her clit because I desperately need her to come. Need to feel her pussy squeeze and pulse around my dick.

"Goddamn, you feel good. So fucking perfect," I tell her. "I need to feel you come, Temple. I need you coming all over my dick. You getting close?"

"Yes," she hisses through her teeth.

"That's it, be my good girl and come."

And she does. Her back arches off the bed and her head tilts back, her face etched with ecstasy. "Flynn! Oh my God!"

Her inner walls pulse and tighten around my cock. "Can I come inside of you, Angel?"

"Yes, do it!"

I let go, slamming home and pouring myself into her. I hold us together for a few more minutes as our bodies recover from the intensity.

"I knew we'd be explosive together," I say.

"You did?" she asks. She reaches out and I thread our fingers together. "How did you know?"

"Because just kissing you makes me hard as a stone. You just do it for me."

"You do it for me too."

chapter thirteen

TEMPLE

The following morning we're called down to join Grandma in the sunroom for breakfast. She's more lucid than I've seen her in a long time, and just being with her floods me with sweet memories from my childhood. She teases with Flynn and he never misses a beat, being his effortlessly charming self.

When we're all done and the kitchen staff has cleared all the tables, Grandma dismisses everyone. She grabs my hand, her grip firm and steady.

"Stay with me a moment, my sweet girl. Flynn, I insist that you treat my Temple like a princess," she says. Her tone is playful, but there's no missing the serious intention behind her words.

"I give you my word that I will. She's my Angel." He kisses Grandma on the cheek, then I get a brief kiss to my lips, and he leaves the room.

"Stephens," Grandma says.

Our family attorney's steps halt and he turns to face her. "Ma'am?"

"You know what to do now," she says.

His eyes land on me and he nods. "Yes, ma'am. I'll take care of it this morning."

"Grandmother?" Rick says from the other side of the table. He seems reluctant to leave the room.

"You are dismissed, Richard. I will speak to you later. Right now, it's Temple's turn."

He shoots me a glare, then finally shuffles out of the room.

"He always was so needy. Even as a child. Of course his mother was the same way. Not at all like you, my dear." Again she squeezes my hand. Her eyes are bright and focused.

"I just wanted to be strong like you," I tell her.

"I know. I am so pleased and relieved to see

you and your husband together. He is very handsome."

I smile. "He definitely is."

"It's been my wish your entire life that you'd find someone who saw you for the special girl you are. Lord knows your parents never did; God rest their souls." She takes a sip of water, her hand shaking as it lifts the glass, then returns it. "Your cousin has been trying to convince me that your marriage is a sham."

I open my mouth to respond, but she shakes her head.

"Hush, let me say my piece before my mind slips. I never know when it's going to happen."

I nod, wiping at my eyes because I can't even imagine how it must feel to know your memory is fading.

"I've instructed Stephens to put you back as executor of my estate. I know you will follow my wishes. Allowing me to live the rest of my days here in this house that I love so much. When I am gone, you can do what you want with it."

The tears are coming stronger now, but I just let them fall. Grief works its way out of your body one way or another; it's futile to try to fight it.

"The marriage thing was just my way to make sure you and Richard had lives. That you'd love and be loved in return. I've seen the way Flynn looks at you, and I have no doubt that he wholeheartedly loves you."

I want to argue. To tell her he doesn't, but that I hope someday he might. But she continues talking.

"Go and live with your husband. Build your life. Start your own family. Come back here and see me now and again. But I am at peace knowing no one is going to take my home away from me while I'm still physically on this Earth."

"Never," I say. "Are you sure you don't want me to move back here until..." I let my words fade, unable to speak the rest of my question.

"Absolutely not. Flynn told me all about that dog sanctuary he and his Army friends are running. What a marvelous thing. And you have always been charmed by the idea of small-town life. That is where you belong. That is the life you're meant to have. At that man's side. Go and live it."

I lean forward and wrap my arms around my grandmother's frail frame. "I love you, Grandma."

"I know you do, sweet girl. I also instructed Stephens to send immediate funds to the dog sanctuary. That kind of endeavor deserves to be a success."

"Thank you. I know Flynn and the rest of the guys will truly appreciate it."

"It is my pleasure. Now, if you don't mind, I'd like to ring for my nurse. I'm feeling tired and need to rest up before the party this evening."

"Of course."

chapter fourteen

FLYNN

The birthday party is over. Temple's grandmother was lucid enough to enjoy about an hour before she became too tired and went to bed.

My girl had returned to me from breakfast, teary-eyed, but happy. Clearly sad at the fact that her grandmother doesn't have a lot of time left, but relieved to once again be executor of the estate. Knowing that her cousin can't displace their grandmother gave Temple so much peace.

Temple is somewhere finalizing last minute payment issues with the caterer, so I'm left to my own devices. I wander around the backyard, which frankly looks like something out of a fairy tale book. Shaped topiaries and perfectly trimmed hedges line the walkways. Every now and then there will be a sculpture or statue you'd swear came from a museum.

To say the Thornes have money would be an understatement. I've never asked where the money comes from, but if I had to guess I'd say old oil. That kind of fortune is the most common in this part of Houston.

"There you are," a woman's voice purrs from behind me. Talon-like nails scrape over my bicep. "I was looking for you."

I turn to face Rick the Dick's wife, Lotus.

I take a step backwards to remove her hands from my body. "Why are you looking for me?"

"Well, now that we're family, I thought we could get to know each other a little better."

I chuckle. "I don't see any reason we need to get to know each other better."

She smiles. "I knew it. You won't be sticking around with frumpy, hot-mess Temple. I can be very discreet, you know."

I shake my head. "Not what I meant at all."

Her eyes rake over my frame and I suppress a shudder.

"Rick is not very well equipped to please a woman like myself, if you know what I mean. But I bet you're packing some serious heat between your legs, aren't you, big boy?"

"Wow, you are brazen aren't you?"

"That and so much more."

"I actually know all I need to know about you," I say.

Her hand goes to her chest as if she's surprised. It's a not-so-veiled movement to draw my eyes to her tits. But I'm not interested.

"We can learn all kinds of things about one another," she coos. She closes the distance between us, then puts both of her palms on my chest. "There's plenty of privacy in the hedge maze."

I cross my arms over my chest and shake my head. "Not interested."

Her expression wavers. "What?"

"I said I'm not interested in whatever it is that you're offering. Women like you are only ever after one thing."

"You don't know anything about me?" she snaps.

"I know your real name isn't Lotus. Well, your original name, I should say. You did legally change it to Lotus when you were sixteen."

Her thin lips purse. "How did you?" she hisses, not even bothering to finish her question.

"I did some intelligence work in the Army. I have skills. Why would a teenage girl change her name from Meredith to Lotus?" I feign curiosity. "I'm guessing you had aspirations of becoming a stripper or Vegas show girl. Am I close?"

"You're a dick," she says.

"Maybe," I say with a shrug. "But I'm a happily married dick who does not cheat on his wife."

"Asshole," she snaps, then marches away from me.

"Thank you for saying that to her," Temple's voice comes from behind me.

I turn to find my wife. "I meant it." I cup her cheek and she leans into my touch.

Then a look of sheer determination covers her face. She grabs my hand and leads me further into the yard.

"Where are we going?" I ask.

"You'll see."

She pulls me towards the hedge maze, and

then inside it. We enter deeper, but she seems to know where she's going. Finally we get to a dead end, but it's a cozy little spot with a stone bench and a climbing flowering vine behind it. She pushes me down until I sit on the bench.

Then she gets on her knees in front of me, her body wedging between my thighs.

"What are you doing, wife?"

Her pretty blue eyes look up at me, but her hands go straight to the button and zipper of my trousers. Then her hand is pulling my erection out of my boxers. She tucks the waistband under my balls.

She reaches for me, and when her hand wraps around my cock, I nearly forget how to breathe. Her tongue swipes out, licking me. Right at the tip. Just a soft, slow taste.

"Fuck—" I swear and lean back against the hedge wall. My attempt to give her more room, more access, more *everything*

"Ah, Angel, you don't have to—"

She meets my gaze and cocks one brow at me. "Flynn, be quiet." Her voice is stern, wicked, and laced with heat. Like a naughty schoolteacher. "I don't want to hear another word unless it's to guide or praise me. Understood?"

I smile. Can't help it. This woman has no idea how she undoes me. I nod. "Yes, ma'am."

She keeps her wide eyes locked on mine as she leans forward and takes the tip of me into her mouth. Her lips stretch around the fat head. I thread my fingers into her soft hair, fisting it on instinct. Not to control her. Just to *feel* her. To know this isn't a dream, or a fantasy I've been nursing since she showed up on my porch with that damn diamond ring and her sweet, sweet smile.

Her hand wraps around the base of me, her fingers barely able to meet, as she swallows more of my dick. Her lips and tongue move in slow, torturous movements. Then she moans, the vibrations rocking through me, and I return the noise.

"You're enjoying this, aren't you, wife? Look at you with your pretty mouth wrapped around me like that. I bet you're soaked between your thighs. Aren't you?"

She whimpers and gives a slight nod but doesn't release my cock. Her cheeks hollow as she sucks me harder.

"Goddamn, Temple. Your mouth feels incredible. I'm not going to last.

She licks at a bead of precum, then keeps working me with her mouth, swirling her tongue and pumping her hand. My hips buck upwards. I can't help it. I don't want to choke her, but the urge to fuck is too strong.

"Temple, love, you... oh God, that feels amazing. Don't fucking stop."

She wasn't going to stop. I knew that. I could see it in the determined look in her eyes. In fact, she slips her free hand beneath her skirt, and I know exactly what she's doing. My whole body shudders.

"Angel, are you touching yourself?" I ask, already knowing the answer. "Do you have any idea how sexy that is? That sucking my cock is turning you on? You're a goddamn fantasy come to life, do you know that?"

She moans—*moans, long and loud*—and the vibration nearly sends me over the edge.

"Are you soaked?" I ask.

She nods, mouth still full of me, eyes still locked on mine.

"I want you to come with me. Can you do that, Angel? Can you make yourself come?"

Another moan. Another swirl of her tongue. She's working herself in rhythm with her hand on me. She's getting close; I see it in her face, the tension building in her body.

Her cheeks hollow again. I see goddamn stars.

"Tell me you're close, Temple. Fuck, it's so good. I'm going to come—" I try to ease her mouth off of me, but she shakes her head, taking me even deeper into her throat.

That's all it takes and I'm coming. Spilling down her throat with a groan I don't even try to muffle.

She comes too. Her eyes closed, body trembling, whimpers muffled by my dick in her mouth.

As soon as our climaxes subside, I reach for her. Scoop her up off the ground and cradle her into my lap. She curls into me without hesitation, her breath warm against my neck, her heart beating as fast as mine.

I press my lips to her temple and whisper against her skin, "You're unbelievable."

chapter **fifteen**

TEMPLE

"I think you're pretty remarkable too," I tell him.

"Will it be too cliched for me to tell you how much I love you right after you gave me the best blow job of my life?"

My heart pounds. "I don't know. Is it a truth or a lie?"

His brown eyes search my face, his expression softens. "The absolute truth. I love you, Temple Harrington."

I am helpless against the smile that overtakes my face. "Does that mean you want me to officially change my name to take yours?"

"I don't actually care what other people call you, as long as I can call you mine."

I nod. "Always. I've always been yours, Flynn."

"You asked me, the other day, how you could thank me for always being your hero?"

"I did."

"I have an answer for you," he says.

"Anything," I tell him. "I'll do anything for you."

"Be my wife forever. Have my babies. Grow old with me."

"Yes!" I kiss him and he holds me against his chest. "Does that mean you'll let me call you Piglet's daddy?"

He leans away from me and gives me a funny look.

"I saw your expression at the festival when I said it. You didn't look too happy," I say.

"I wasn't unhappy. It turned me on. The thought of being a daddy with you. Then I thought of getting you pregnant, having a baby with you. I was just aroused at all of those thoughts."

That makes me laugh. "So you do want kids?"

"I want anything and everything, as long as you're the one by my side."

"Right now, I want you to take me back inside and make love to me again," I say.

"You don't have to ask me twice."

"I love you, Flynn," I say. "In case it wasn't obvious already."

"So I guess this is what stupid in love looks like," he says.

"Yeah. I guess so."

epilogue

FLYNN

A few months later...

"Angel? Where are you?" I call when I step into our cabin. It's not like there are many places for her to be; it's a small place. We're currently building our dream home out on some land not too far from Great Dane's. But in the meantime, it's just me and my girl and our son, as Temple so often likes to refer to Piglet.

I pretend it bothers me sometimes just because it usually leads to Temple doing dirty things to me.

"Temple?" I call again.

That's when I hear the shower running. I step inside the bathroom to find my wife singing a Jess Munoz song. Piglet is curled up on Temple's discarded clothes on the bathroom floor.

"Angel."

She squeals. "You scared me." She pokes a wet head out of the side of the shower curtain to shoot me a glare.

"Need any help washing anything?" I ask.

She rolls her eyes. "No, I'm almost done."

"Have we had any deliveries yet today?"

"I don't think so. At least nothing before I got in here. Why? You expecting something?"

"I am. I ordered you a surprise."

The water shuts off and she pulls the towel hanging over the shower curtain rod into the tub with her.

I'm just about to tell her she better not be covering up any of my favorite parts of her when she slides the curtain out of the way. She's still gloriously naked. Water droplets cling to her every curve. But her hair is wrapped up in the aforementioned towel—turban style.

She tilts her head and smiles. "What did you get me?"

"It's a surprise," I say.

"Well, that's no fun. Anything I can do to convince you to tell me?"

I pull her wet body against me, my hands instinctively going down to squeeze her ass. "We might can think of something."

She leans up, licking a hot trail up my neck. Then her teeth are nibbling at my ear lobe.

"It's a replacement vibe for the one we left in that hotel shower," I say.

"Oh, good. I really liked that one. Maybe I should stop using them in showers though."

"Where's the fun in that?" I ask. "Let's go to the bedroom."

"Okay," Temple says.

Our doorbell rings.

"Oh, perfect timing. Go grab our new toy," she says, then she walks across the small hallway to our bedroom.

I open the door expecting to find a delivery man and instead find my sister.

"Daisy! Long time no see." I pull her into an embrace, and she immediately bursts into tears. "Hey Angel," I call over my shoulder. "Put some clothes on, we have company."

"Who is it?" Temple yells.

"It's Daisy."

"Daisy!" she squeals.

I've got my sister on the couch with a bottle of water by the time my wife makes it out to her.

"I have missed you so much," Temple says as she comes forward and embraces Daisy.

Daisy sniffles. "I'm so sorry I missed your grandmother's funeral. I wanted to be here. I tried."

Temple's brow furrows. "Hey, do not think another moment about it. You're here now, that's what matters."

Daisy looks between me and Temple. "I can't believe y'all are all in love and married."

"We are," I say, reaching across to squeeze my wife's knee.

"You both deserve to be happy."

I know something is bothering my sister, something more than missing a funeral. For a moment I'm worried she has more of a problem with mine and Temple's relationship than she's let on

"I have news," she says. Another sniff. "I'm pregnant." Then comes a sob.

"Sweetie," Temple coos. "Why is that sad? Or

is it just hormones? Babies are not always timely, but they're always a blessing."

"It's not the baby. It's that I have to do it all alone." Daisy blows out a breath. "Turns out my perfect British boyfriend wasn't so perfect at all. He'd been separated from his wife, divorce papers in hand. At least that's what he told me."

I stand to pace, to give the anger surging through me somewhere to go. "Do you want me to kill him?" I ask. "I can make it look like an accident."

Daisy gives a watery laugh. "No. He's not worth it. He went back to his wife. She's pregnant too, it seems. He gave me a lump sum amount of cash for a trust fund for the baby, signed off on his parental rights, and paid for me to come back home."

"You don't worry about a thing," Temple says. "We've got you."

Another doorbell. I walk over to the door and take the package from the delivery guy. I close the door, then hold up the box. "Guess it's good this came after my sister showed up." Then I wink at my wife.

. . .

***

I hope you loved Flynn and Temple's story. Please consider **leaving me a review**.

Read the other books in the Dog Tags series:

Jack of Hearts
Fools Rush Flynn
Quid Pro Beau
Love 'em or Liam
Happily Evan After
Ready, Willing and Abel
Romero and Juliette

Grab **Redeem My Heart** if you want to see where Great Dane's Dog Sanctuary started.

Keep scrolling for an excerpt from **Lone Star Husband**, another marriage of convenience story set in Saddle Creek.

thank you for reading!

Join my newsletter for bonus epilogues, deleted scenes and a FREE BOOK.

join me!

COME JOIN my **VIP Reader Group on Facebook** where I do sneak peeks, answer questions and keep you up to date with everyone going on in Kat Baxter land.

excerpt from lone star husband

HARRISON

I'm the fourth of six and I'm a twin. I grew up never having anything that was just my own. To this day, I still live on the ranch that I run with two of my brothers. I love the ranch—and my brothers when they aren't being dumbasses. I'd do anything for my family but there are times when I crave solitude. Especially when I have a problem that needs solving.

Which is why I made this trip from Saddle Creek to Houston by myself. I needed time to think. Time to plan.

It's been less than two full weeks since we found out that our grandfather has some crazy shit written into his will. The old man—much like Voldemort himself—is too mean to die without a fight. Although, he's had a stroke, which means that day might not be too far off. Our asshole uncle—whom we call Uncle Umbridge—didn't want us to know any of this. Why? Because if our grandfather dies before we're married—with prenups he approves of—our land could go to Uncle Umbridge.

If it was simply a matter of finding someone to marry, I could do that. Don't get me wrong, I don't want to jump into marriage just to satisfy the requirements of my grandfather's will, but I could.

Except I can't.

Because I'm already married.

It's a long story. One I haven't shared with anyone in my family, except my brother Roe. It was Roe who suggested I skip town without telling the rest of the Crawford clan about my marriage, that I talk to Birdie first and figure out where she's at before I spill the beans to the rest of the jackals.

Don't get me wrong. I love my family. Even the ones who piss me off most of the time. But, sometimes, I need for them to not be up in my business.

I'm thankful as fuck I made the right choice in confiding my secret to Roe. It's given me a blissful twelve hours of silence. The entire drive from Saddle Creek to Houston, and my night in the hotel.

I could've tried to get in touch with Birdie last night. I have her address and her phone number. But I just needed the time by myself to figure out how the hell I'm going to handle this.

Seeing my wife after eight months is weird

because not only do I know next to nothing about her, but she's also my wife in name only.

What I do know is that she's from Saldania, which is some tiny country in the North Sea near Finland. I'd never even heard of it and had to look it up on Google Maps. Mike, my best friend growing up, was having trouble getting Birdie's work visa renewed because her parents are diplomats and had arranged a marriage for her back home.

I would've helped just because Mike asked, but finding out what I did about her situation sealed the deal. No grown-ass woman in the modern world should have her career hamstrung because her parents are trying to arrange a marriage for her. That's bullshit, no matter where you're from.

So I stepped in to help. Eight months ago, I told my brothers and sister I was visiting Mike for the weekend, drove down to Houston, and married Birdie seventeen minutes after meeting her for the first time. Less than twenty-four hours later, I was back in Saddle Creek, and I haven't seen or spoken to her since.

Now I'm sitting in my truck, parked in the multi-level parking garage near Mike's office. My phone has been vibrating with incoming messages for the last fifteen minutes. Clearly, my siblings are now all aware of why I've left town.

I open my messages to our group text that my sister annoying named, "The Jolly Ranchers."

MADISON: So are we not gonna talk about the fact that Harrison left town to go get his WIFE?

MADISON: His WIFE!!!

JOHNNY: Wait, what?

HAYES: In a meeting, so I'm muting y'all.

MADISON: <gif of the Olson twins rolling their eyes>

MADISON: Do you think he even read my original text and realizes his twin brother is married?

QUINN: Did anyone know?

ROE: He told me before he left town. Mostly because he knew y'all would ask questions.

QUINN: Obviously that's why he didn't tell Mad. She would've had 172 questions.

MADISON: As if y'all don't have them too. I mean seriously? How has he kept this from us? Where is she? How did they meet? How long have they been married?

JOHNNY: Exactly. I want to know everything too. Damn. About to take a test though so I'm going dark.

ME: I will answer y'all's questions when I get home.

MADISON: OMG! Harrison? Are you with her now? What's her name? Can we have a picture?

QUINN: Jesus, Mad, this is why no one talks to you.

MADISON: <emoji of middle finger>

ME: Patience, Mad. I'll either show you a picture or you'll be meeting her soon.

With that, I silence and pocket my phone, then get out of my truck. I glance down at myself and wonder if I should've dressed up more. The truth is, I'm a simple cowboy. I married her to help her with a situation and now I need her to reciprocate. So it shouldn't matter if I'm wearing jeans and a t-shirt.

I already know that my buddy, Mike, isn't in the office because he's traveling to some gaming con.

Plus, I'm not here to see him.

I get off the elevator on the floor for PenDragon Games and find myself facing a large reception desk. As I exit the elevator, a woman nearly runs straight into me. She skitters back a step, like my very presence startled her. I'm a big motherfucker, despite my efforts to change some of that. I can't do a damn thing about my height, but I did try diets and eating salads for a while to try to slim my waistline.

Nothing worse than being one half of a set of fraternal twins and you're known as the "fat one." Hayes, my brother, he would be the "hot one." Whatever. So yeah, I'm a big guy. I'm strong as the proverbial ox and I'm thick everywhere. My oldest brother, Quinn, is sort of built the same, but he has more definition in his abs. I've got abs, they're just under a layer of padding. Or a layer of pudding as my Mama used to say.

Behind the reception desk, there's a massive wall of frosted glass with the company's name and logo etched into it. Behind the desk are two people—a guy with short-cropped bright blue hair, and a petite woman with owlish eyes.

I walk up to the desk, tip my hat, and say to the woman, "Excuse me, ma'am."

She blinks up at me, then titters. Probably because she's younger than me and I called her "ma'am." I know my manners are old-fashioned, but it's how I was raised.

"Can I help you?"

"I'm looking for—"

Before I can finish the sentence, the guy elbows his co-worker and steps up to the desk. "Oh, my God. You're Birdie's husband."

The woman looks at him, confused, then back at me.

I clear my throat, uncertain what the right response is here. I didn't tell anyone in Saddle Creek about the wedding and it didn't occur to me that she might have handled things differently on her end.

Understanding dawns on the woman's face. "You are, aren't you?"

I nod, reluctantly.

She titters again, shooting a conspiratorial grin at the guy. “We were beginning to think you weren't real.” She leans in and whispers as if confiding in me. “We actually have an office pool.”

“A what?”

“You know, like a bet. I mean, she has a picture of you in her office from y’all’s wedding. And she talks about you, but no one has ever seen you. And you never call.” She lifts a bony shoulder in a shrug. “We sorta thought you weren't real.”

I stare at the woman, waiting for the punchline because surely that’s not it. Do all of Birdie's colleagues whisper this shit behind her back?

“Some of us thought you were a figment of her imagination,” the woman continues. “She's a strange one, that Birdie.”

I don’t try to hide my glare. “I think ‘creative’ is the word you're looking for. Or perhaps intelligent. My wife is brilliant, and as you can see, I’m not a figment of her imagination.” I hold my arms out to emphasize my size.

The woman eyes me up and down and visibly swallows. “Yes, I do see. Well, she should be in her office.” She scurries around the reception desk and uses a badge to swipe open the door. Gesturing me in, she adds loud enough that others can hear, "Birdie's office is the third door on the left. But since you're her husband, I'm sure you know that."

Offices line the outer rim of the floor, but the center is a weird combination of beanbag chairs, yoga balls, large pillows, and gaming chairs. Seems like everyone is wearing those giant headphones covering their ears.

I nod and walk away, but I can hear the whispers all around me. I glance back over my shoulder and see that the guy from reception has joined the woman, along with two other people, and they're all whispering.

If they hadn't been paying attention before, they sure are now. I wonder if Mike knows how much time his underlings spend gossiping.

The offices that line the bullpen all have big glass windows. So as soon as I spot Birdie's office, I can see her through the window. My steps slow as I drink in the sight of her. Her desk is angled toward the opposite wall, so she doesn't see me. Maybe I should have called or texted her to warn her I was coming.

By the time I reach her office doorway, my

stomach is tied in knots. But there she is, sitting behind her desk looking cute as fuck with a set of pink headphones with cat ears on top of two ash-blonde braids. The walls of her office are plastered in posters. Some are music bands, but others must be for video games because I don't recognize them. The space between her keyboard and the multiple monitors is taken up with dozens of tiny figurines and miniature toys. She's dressed in a vintage Atari shirt that V's deep into her lush cleavage.

Like the first time I laid eyes on my wife, I go rock hard behind my zipper. She hasn't seen me yet, so I just stand there and watch her for a minute as her eyes flick from one of the three monitors in front of her to another. She frowns, then bites down on her lip. Then she nods and reaches for the desk and picks up a partially eaten jelly donut. She takes a bite and a huge glob of red gelatinous filling falls right into her cleavage.

And that's when she looks up and sees me.

Grab **Lone Star Husband**

about the author

USA Today Bestselling Author, Kat Baxter writes fast-paced, sweet & STEAMY romantic comedies. Readers have dubbed her "The Queen of Adorkable." and her books "laugh-out-loud funny," and "hot enough to melt your kindle." She lives in Texas with her family and a menagerie of animals. Kat is the pseudonym for a bestselling historical romance author.

What readers have said about Kat's books:

"Kat Baxter is my catnip!" ~ Goodreads review

"Whenever I need my sexy nerdy dirty talking romance fix, I know Kat Baxter has my back!" ~Goodreads review

"How does Kat Baxter make me fall in love with her characters in just 12 short chapters? It's coz she's a freaken magic weaver with her words!!" ~ Amazon review

"You'll instantly fall in love." ~Goodreads review

"Swoon. I could not get enough of this story and fell in love with both these characters!" ~Amazon review

"... the chemistry between them is instant and off the charts!" ~Amazon review

"... original, hot, and a hoot!" ~Amazon review

"DAMN it's hot." ~Amazon review

"... sweetness, heat and humor. By the time the story was over, my cheeks hurt from smiling so hard." ~Amazon review

"Such a very sweet and spicy story!" ~ Goodreads

"The connection between the characters felt real, and I liked the author's writing style." ~ Goodreads

Made in the USA
Coppell, TX
20 January 2026